ᑕᐃᒃᓱᒪᓂᐊᓗᒃ
WAY BACK THEN

ᑎᑎᕋᖅᑕᑦ
Written by

ᓃᑦ ᑯᕆᔅᑕᕗᒧᑦ
Neil Christopher

ᑎᑎᕋᐅᔭᖅᑕᑦ
Illustrated by

ᔨᕐᒪᐃ ᐊᕐᓇᑦᑕᐅᔪᕐᒧᑦ
Germaine Arnaktauyok

ᓯᕗᒧᐊᒃᑎᑕᖅ Foreword

ᔨᕐᒪᐃᓐ ᐊᕐᓇᑦᑕᐅᔫᑉ ᑎᑎᖅᑐᒐᑦᑎᐊᕚᓗᖏᓐᓂᒃ ᑕᑯᖃᑦᑕᕆᐊᙵᓚᐅᖅᓯᒪᔪᖓ ᒪᑯᒃᑎᓪᓗᖓ ᐃᓕᓴᐃᔨᒃᓴᕈᖅᐸᓪᓕᐊᑎᓪᓗᖓ. ᑕᐃᒃᓯᒪᓂ ᕿᑭᖅᑖᓗᖕᒥᑦ ᐃᓕᓐᓂᐊᖅᑐᓕᕆᔨᕐᔪᐊᒃᑯᑦ ᐅᖃᓕᒫᒐᓕᐅᖅᐸᓚᐅᖅᓯᒪᖕᒪᑕ ᔨᕐᒪᐃᓐᓗ ᑎᑎᖅᑐᒐᖅᓯᒪᔭᖏᓐᓂᒃ ᐱᑕᖃᓚᐅᓪᓚᒃᐸᒃᑐᓂ. ᐃᓕᓴᐃᔨᕈᖅᑎᓪᓗᖓ, ᐅᖃᓕᒫᕆᐊᖓ ᖁᕕᐊᒋᓪᓚᑦᑖᖅᐸᓚᐅᖅᓯᒪᒐᒃᑯ ᐃᓕᓐᓂᐊᖅᑎᖁᑎᓐᓄᑦ ᐅᖃᓕᒫᖅᐸᒃᑐᒋᓪᓗ ᖄᖓᓂᑦ ᑐᓄᐊᓄᑦ ᐊᕐᕌᒍᓕᒫᒥᓪᓗ ᐅᖃᓕᒫᒐᐃᑦ ᓈᕙᒃᑐᑎᒍᓪᓗ. ᐃᓕᓐᓂᐊᖅᑏᑦ ᖁᕕᐊᑦᑕᒃᐸᓚᐅᖅᓯᒪᖕᒪᑕ ᑭᓇ ᐅᖃᓕᒫᒐᓕᐅᕐᓂᕐᒪᖔᑦ ᐊᒻᒪ ᑭᓇ ᑎᑎᖅᑐᒐᕐᓂᕐᒪᖔᑦ ᔨᕐᒪᐃᓐᓗ ᑎᑎᖅᑐᒐᖏᓐᓂᒃ ᐃᓕᓴᖅᓯᔪᓐᓇᖅᓯᓚᐅᖅᓯᒪᖕᒪᑕ. ᔨᕐᒪᐃᓐ ᑎᑎᖅᑐᒐᖕᒥᑦ ᓱᕈᓰᑦ ᑕᑯᓕᒪᔭᖏᓐᓂᒃ ᑎᑎᖅᑐᒐᖅᓯᒪᕙᓚᐅᖅᓯᒪᖕᒪᑕ. ᑮᓇᖏᑕ ᑕᒃᑯᖏᑦ ᐊᓐᓄᕌᙳᐊᖏᓪᓗ ᓱᕈᓯᕐᓄᑦ ᐃᓕᙵᔭᐅᓚᐅᖅᓯᒪᔪᑦ.

I was first exposed to Germaine Arnaktauyok's wonderful illustrations when I was a young teacher trainee. Books published by the Baffin Divisional Board of Education occasionally featured Germaine's illustrations. She quickly grew to be my favourite artist. When I became a teacher, I loved reading Inuktitut books to my students, and we read all the board's Inuktitut books from cover to cover in a school year. The children would get excited about who had written

and illustrated the books, and they became familiar with Germaine's work through these books. Germaine's illustrations contained characters that the children recognized. All the features and the attire of the characters were what the children were familiar with.

ᐅᐊᑦᑎᐊᕈᒃᑲᓐᓂᐅᓕᖅᑎᑦᑐᒍ, ᐊᖏᔪᖅᖑᖅ ᑎᑎᖅᑐᒐᖅᓯᒪᔪᓂᒃ ᐊᑭᓐᓇᖅᒥᐅᑕᖅᑲᓚᐅᖅᓯᒪᖕᒪᑦ ᔨᖅᒪᐃᓐ ᑎᑎᖅᑐᒐᖅᑕᕝᓂᖕᒋᓐᓂᒃ. ᔨᖅᒪᐃᓐ ᓄᑲᓇᖕᒪᒍ. ᐱᑖᓇᐊᖅᑲᓂᓚᐅᖅᓯᒪᔪᖕᒐ ᐱᐅᒋᒧᑦ ᑎᑎᖅᑐᒐᐃᑦ. ᔨᖅᒪᐃᓐ ᑎᑎᖅᑐᒐᖅᓯᒪᔭᖕᒋᓐᓂᒃ ᓄᐊᑦᑎᖅᑲᑦᑕᓂᓚᐅᖅᓯᒪᒋᕗᖕᒐ ᓴᓇᓯᒪᔪᓂᒃ ᐅᓂᒃᑳᖅᑐᐊᓂᒃ ᑐᓵᖅᑲᑦᑕᖅᓯᒪᔭᒪ ᐃᓚᖕᒋᓐᓂᒃ. ᒪᖅᕘᒃ ᑎᑎᖅᑐᑳᒃ ᐱᐅᒋᓂᖅᐹᖅᔭᐊᒃᑲ ᓄᓇᐅᑉ ᖅᑭᑐᖅᖓᖕᒋᑦ ᐊᒻᒪ ᐅᐃᓂᒍᒪᓇᓂ ᐅᔭᖅᑲᕈᖅᑐᕝᓂᖅ.

Later on, my *angijurnguq* (sister-in-law) at the time, who is Germaine's sister, put up framed prints of Germaine's work in her house. I wanted to get some prints for myself, as I loved her work. I started collecting Germaine's art, especially the work that draws inspiration from the oral legends that I grew up listening to. My two favourite pieces are depictions of the earth children and the woman who turned to stone because she did not want to marry.

ᖁᕕᐊᔪᑦᑎᐊᖅᑯᖕᒪ ᐅᓇ ᐅᖃᓕᒫᒡᖅ ᓴᓇᔭᐅᑎᑦᑐᒍ ᐱᖅᑲᐅᔾᖁᓇᑕᐅᖅᒐᒻ.
ᖁᕕᐊᒥᓂᐊᖅᐸᑎᑐᖅ ᐅᓂᒃᑲᑦ ᐅᕇᑎᖁᓄᑦ ᑐᖕᖅᑲᐅᑎᑕᑦ. ᐅᓂᒃᑲᑦ
ᓇᐃᑦᑎᖅᕆᒪᒐᕐ ᖁᕕᐊᒥᓂᐊᖅᐸᑎᑐᖅ ᑐᑭᓴᓂᐊᖅᖐᑦ ᐃᓄᐃᑦ
ᐅᓂᒃᑲᖅᑐᐊᖕᖐᓂᒃ ᐊᒻᒪᓗ ᖁᕕᐊᒥᓗᒢᑦ ᑎᑎᖅᑐᒡᕐᖿᒪᒐᕐ ᒋᖅᑯᓂᖕᒪ
ᐱᙳᖅᑎᑕᒡᕐᖿᒐᕐᕐ.

I am so excited to have been involved in the creation of this
book. I hope you will enjoy the short glimpse of each story shared.
These stories will help you to understand our rich Inuit oral tradition.
I also hope you enjoy the drawings themselves, as they make these
stories come to life.

ᖁᕕᐊᒥᓂᐊᖅᐸᑎᑐᖅ
Qujannamiik,

ᑐᐃᔅ ᖄᑦᕼᐅᕐᑎ
Louise Flaherty

Inuktitut Pronunciation Guide

angijurnguq — Older brother-in-law or older sister-in-law, pronounced "ang-nee-yo-nook."

ataata — Father, pronounced "a-ta-ta."

atii — A term meaning "let's go," or "let's do it," pronounced "a-tee."

iglu — A traditional snow house, pronounced "ig-loo."

igluit — Many iglus, pronounced "ig-loo-eet."

kuluit — A term of endearment meaning "dear ones," pronounced "koo-loo-eet."

nanurluk — A giant polar bear, pronounced "nan-oor-look."

ningiuq — Grandmother or old woman, pronounced "ning-yook."

qulliq — A seal-oil lamp, pronounced "koo-lik."

Tuniit — The people who lived in the Arctic before Inuit, pronounced "too-neet."

“ᐊᑖᑖᒃ, ᓯᓂᒍᓐᓇᐃᑦᓕᒐᑦᑕ. ᐅᓂᒃᑳᖅᑐᐊᕇᑦ?” ᒪᒃᐸ ᐊᐱᕆᕗᖅ.

“ᐊᑏ, ᐃᒻᒪᑲᑦᓚᒃᓯᐅᑎᙳᐊᓂᒃ ᐅᓂᒃᑳᓚᐅᕆᑦ,” ᓇᐃᓚ ᐊᐱᕆᕗᖅ.

“ᐃᒻᒪᑲᑦᓚᒃᓯᐅᑎᓃᒃ? ᖃᓄᖅ, ᓄᑲᑉᐱᐊᑯᓘᑎᑦᑐᙶ?” ᑲᑦᓗᒃ ᐊᐱᕆᕗᖅ.

“ᐋᒃᑲ,” ᓇᐃᓚ ᑭᐅᑦᑐᓂ. “ᐃᒻᒪᑲᑦᓚᒃ ᖃᖅᑳᓗᐃᑦ ᐊᖏᔪᐊᓘᑎᑦᑐᒋᑦ ᐊᒻᒪ ᓄᓇᖅᔪᐊᖅ ᑕᐸᓇᐃᑦᑐᐊᓘᑎᑦᑐᒍ.”

The night was growing late, and Kudlu’s children were not yet sleeping. So he sat down beside them on the sleeping platform and whispered, “*Kuluit*, why are you still awake?”

“We cannot sleep, *Ataata*. Please tell us a story!” Makpa asked.

“Yes, please tell us about what things were like long ago,” Nyla added.

“A story about long ago? Do you mean when I was a boy?” Kudlu asked.

ᑲᑦᑐᒃ ᖅᑐᖅᖕᒐᓂ ᖅᐱᐊᖅᐸᐊᑦ, ᖅᑯᖕᒪᔾᑐᓂ ᐅᖅᑲᖅᐳᖅ.
"ᐅᓂᒃᑲᐅᔾᕈᐱᒥᕏᔾ ᐃᒻᒪᑲᑕᓪᖁᐳᑎᖕᒐᑐᓂᖅ? ᐊᑎᑦ,
ᐃᖅᑲᖅᓱᕆᔪᖕᒐᓂᐊᖅᐸᒃ ᓂᖕᒋᐅᖕᒐ
ᐅᓂᑲᖅᐸᓗᐅᖅᕐᒪᕐᓂᒐᑎᒃ ᐃᒻᒪᑲᑕᓪᖁᐳᑎᑦ."

ᑕᖅᑲᖑᖁ ᐊᓄᑎᕉᑦᑎᒪᔪᖅᑎᑦᑐᒍ ᐊᒻᒪ
ᓂᒃᑕᖅᐸᑦᑕᐊᑐᐃᖑᕋᔪᖅᑎᑦᑐᒍ,
ᐃᒃᑐᒥᑕ ᐃᓗᐊᓂ ᐅᖅᑯᕐᔪᖅ ᐊᒻᒪ ᑲᖕᒐᖅᖁᑐᓂ.
ᖅᑯᑦᑕᐅᑦ ᖅᑲᐅᒪᖁᒪ ᐃᒃᑐᖁᑦ ᐊᑭᖑᖑᒐᓂ ᖅᑲᐅᒪᒃᖁᕈᐅᖅ
ᑕᖅᖅᑲᖅᑎᑎᑐᓂᑐ. ᖅᑐᖅᒪᖁᑎᑦ ᖅᐱᑎᐊᖅᑲᖑᓂᖅᒪᑕ, ᑲᑦᑐᒃ
ᐅᓂᒃᑲᖅᑐᐊᕐᒐᐊᖅᐳᖅ.

"No, Ataata," Nyla answered. "I want to hear about when the mountains were giants and there was lots of magic in the world."

Kudlu looked at his two children and smiled. "Oh, you want a story about way back then? *Atii*, I will try to remember the stories my *ningiuq* used to tell about that time."

Although the wind could be heard whistling outside and the temperature was dropping, it was warm and cozy inside the *iglu*. The *qulliq*'s soft light danced across the snow walls of their home. The children pulled their blankets close, and Kudlu began his story.

ᐃᒻᒪᑲᓪᓛᓘᑎᓪᓗᒍ ᓯᓚ ᓄᓇᕐᔪᐊᖅ ᓄᑖᙳᑎᓪᓗᒍ, ᑭᓯᓚᒦᑦ ᐊᔾᔨᒌᓚᐅᙱᑕᙵᑦ ᐅᓪᓗᒥᑎᑐᑦ. ᑕᐅᑐᙳᐊᕐᓇᙱᑦᑐᕐᓘᓃᑦ ᖃᓄᐃᑦᑑᓚᐅᖅᓯᒪᓂᖓ, ᐅᓐᓄᐊᖅᑲᓚᐅᖅᓯᒪᙱᒻᒪᑦ ᐅᓪᓗᖅᑐᖅᑲᙱᖢᓂᓗ.

ᓯᓚ ᓱᕋᓚᐅᖅᓯᒪᙱᕐᖢᓂ ᐊᕐᔾᔭᖓᐃᓐᓇᐅᔭᓚᐅᖅᓯᒪᔪᖅ.

ᑎᕆᒐᓂᐊᑯᓗᒃᑕᖅᑲᓚᐅᖅᓯᒪᔪᖅ ᑖᖅᓯᖅᑲᑦᑕᕐᑯᔾᔪᕆᒃ ᐊᓯᒥᓂ ᑎᒃᑕᒐᖅᑲᑦᑕᕈᒪᒐᒥ ᑕᑯᔭᐅᙱᓪᓗᓂ. ᑖᓐᓇ ᑎᕆᒐᓂᐊᖅ ᐊᖓᒃᑯᖁᓘᒐᒥ ᓯᓚ ᑖᖅᓯᕐᑯᕚ, ᑕᐃᒪᐃᓕᖓᓪᓗ ᓯᓚ ᑖᖅᓯᒋᖅ ᐅᓐᓄᒃᖢᓂᓗ. ᑕᐃᒪᐃᓕᑎᓪᓗᒍ ᖁᓚᐅᑦᑐᖅᑲᖅᐳᖅ ᑐᓗᒐᕐᒥᒃ, ᑖᖅᑎᓪᓗᒍᓗ ᓂᕿᑦᓴᖅᓯᐅᕈᓐᓇᙱᖢᓂ ᐱᙳᐊᕈᑎᒃᓴᖅᓯᐅᕈ ᓐᓇᙱᕐᖢᓂᓗ. ᑖᖅᑎᓪᓗᒍ ᓱᔪᓐᓇᙱᓐᓇᒥ, ᑐᓗᒐᖅ ᓯᓚᒥᒃ ᖃᐅᒻᒪᖁᔾᔪᕗᖅ. ᑕᐃᒪᐃᓕᖓᒻᒪᑦ ᖃᐅᒻᒪᒃᐳᖅ ᐅᓪᓗᙳᖅᖢᓂᓗ.

ᑖᒃᑯᐊᒃ ᓂᕐᔫᑏᒃ ᐊᖏᖅᑲᑎᒌᙳᓐᓇᙱᓐᓂᖏᓐᓄᑦ ᐅᓪᓗᒥ
ᐅᓪᓗᖅᑲᖅᐳᒍᑦ
ᐅᓐᓄᐊᖅᑲᖅᐳᒍᓪᓗ.

Way back then, when the world was very, very young, things were different than they are today. It is hard to imagine that time, as there was no night and day.

There was only a grey sky that never changed.

One day, a fox wanted darkness so it could steal from others without being seen. This fox was full of magic, so when it asked the sky for darkness, it became night. Just then, a raven was flying by, and it needed light to find food and things to play with. The dark sky was not good for the raven, so it asked for light. Then the sky brightened, and it became day.

Because these two animals could never agree, we now have day and night.

ᐃᒻᒪᑲᓪᓚᒃ ᓄᓇ ᑐᒃᑐᖃᓚᐅᖅᓯᒪᙱᑦᑐᖅ. ᐃᓄᐃᑦ ᐊᖑᓇᓱᑐᐃᓐᓇᖅᐸᓚᐅᖅᓯᒪᔪᑦ ᓂᕐᔪᑎᐊᓛᓂᒃ, ᐊᒻᒪ ᑭᓱᑐᐃᓐᓇᕐᓂᒃ ᓂᕆᔪᓐᓇᖅᑕᒥᓂᒃ, ᐊᓪᓛᑦᓘᓐᓃᑦ ᐃᔾᔪᑦ ᐅᔭᖅᑲᑦᓗ. ᑐᒃᑐᐃᑦ ᓄᓇᐅᑉ ᐃᑭᐊᖓᓂ ᓄᓇᖃᖅᐸᓚᐅᖅᓯᒪᔪᑦ, ᐊᖑᓇᓱᒃᑕᐅᔪᓐᓇᙱᔅᓱᑎᓪᓗ ᑕᑯᔭᐅᔪᓐᓇᙱᓐᓇᒥᒃ.

ᓄᓇᐅᑉ ᐃᓄᐊ ᓄᓕᐊᒥᓂᒃ ᑐᒃᑐᖁᔨᔅᓴᓕᕐᒥ ᓄᓇ ᖁᓚᐃᑉᐹ, ᑐᒃᑐᑦᓗ ᐊᓂᑎᔅᓱᓂᑦ.
ᓯᕗᓪᓕᕐᒥᒃ ᐊᑕᐅᓯᕐᒥᒃ ᒪᕐᕈᐃᓐᓈᖕᓂᓪᓘᓐᓃᑦ ᐊᓂᑦᑎᓚᐅᖅᓯᒪᔪᖅ, ᑭᓯᐊᓂᓗ ᐱᔮᓇᙱᓱᓂ ᓄᓇᒥᒃ ᒪᑐᐃᙵᖅᑎᑦᑏᓐᓇᓕᕐᓂᕐᒪᑦ ᐊᒥᓱᐊᓗᐃᑦ ᑐᒃᑐᑦ
ᐊᓂᓚᐅᖅᓯᒪᔪᑦ.

ᓄᓇᐅᑉ ᐃᓄᐊ ᓄᓇᒥᒃ ᖁᓚᐃᑦᑎᓚᐅᕐᓂᖓᓄᑦ, ᐅᑭᐅᖅᑕᖅᑐᒥ ᐊᒥᓱᐊᓗᖕᓂᒃ ᑐᒃᑐᖃᓕᖅᐳᑦ.

Way back then, there were no caribou on the land. People hunted only small animals, and almost everything could be eaten, even dirt and rocks. The caribou we now depend on lived underground, safely away from hunters.

But one day, a land spirit who wanted to provide for his wife cut a hole into the earth and let the caribou out. At first he only let out one or two caribou, but the hole was accidentally left open and many, many caribou escaped.

And now, because of this land spirit's action, the North is filled with caribou.

ᐃᒻᒪᒃᑳᓪᒃ ᓂᕐᔪᑏᑦ ᐊᒥᖅᓂᒃ ᓱᓗᖕᒥᓂᓘᖅᐅᑦ ᐱᖅᓱᔭᕈᓇᑕᐅᖅᔪᒪᖁᑦ,
ᓲᖅᓗ ᑖᒪᖁᓇ ᐊᖁᓇᖃᐅᔭᖅᐸᖃᑦᑕ. ᐊᒥᖅᓂᒃ ᓱᓗᖕᒥᓂᓗ
ᐱᖅᓱᔭᕋᖕᒥᑕ ᐃᓄᑐᐃᓐᓇᐅᖅᑯᔾᐯᖃᑕᐅᖅᑐᑦ. ᐅᓂᒃᒃᑐᐊᑐᖅᓅᒥ
ᐊᖕᐅᑎᖅᑲᑕᐅᓯᓂᖅᐳᖅ
ᑲᖕᔪᖅᔭᐊᓯᓂᖕᒥᒃ ᑖᗅᑯᓘᒥ ᐳᐃᖕᔪᖅᑐᒥ. ᓱᓗᖕᒥᓂᒃ ᐱᖅᓱᒪᒪᒥ
ᐊᖅᐊᑕᖅᐊᕿᓗᖕᔪᑕᐅᖅᓱᒪᒪᖅ. ᑖᖃ ᐊᖁᑦ ᑲᖕᔪᒥᒃ ᐊᖅᐊᒥᒃ ᐊᐱᑎᕈᖅ
ᓄᓪᐊᖅᑕᖅᔾᒪᓂᖃᖅᒃᒍᓂᐅᒃ. ᐊᖅᔭᒧᒃᔪᓂᒪᒃ ᑖᕐᓯᒥᖕᒪ ᐅᐃᖃᑲᑐᖅᐳᖅ.
        ᑖᓛᐃᑑᖕᔾᐊᖅᓅᒥ ᑖᖃ ᑲᖕᔪᖅ ᐃᖕᑭᐊᖕᔾᑐᖅᐳᖅ ᓲᒃᖁᒃᓗ
ᖃᖕᑳᑕᒃᓪᖕᒃᑎᖅᓅᒥ. ᐅᐃᒥᓂ ᐃᖕᔭᖅᑐᖅᓅᒥ ᐊᖑᑦᑕᐅᑎᖅᐳᖅ
ᓱᓗᖕᓂᒃ ᓴᓇᔭᖕᒪᕿᒃ. ᑖᖃ ᐊᖁᑎ ᐊᖅᐅᒥᐅᒃ,
ᑲᖕᔾᖕᖕᒃᖃᖕᓂᖅᐳᖅ ᑎᖕᒃᓅᓅ.

Way back then, animals could remove their fur or feathers like we remove clothing. When they took off their animal skins, they would appear human underneath. In an old story, a man found a snow goose swimming in a small lake. Without her feathers, she was a beautiful woman, so he asked this goose-woman to be his wife. She was with the man for several years.

In time, the goose began to miss flying. So one day, in secret, she made a new jacket of feathers. When she put on this feather jacket, she became a goose once again and flew away.

ᐃᒻᒪᒃᑦᑕᖖᒍᓄᒃ ᐅᑭᐅᖅᑕᖅᑐᖅ ᐃᓄᑭᑦᑐᑯᓗᒡᑕᐅᖅᕐᒪᓚᐅᖅᖅ. ᐃᓄᐃᑦ
ᐅᓄᖅᕐᓯᑲᖃᓂᕐᑰᓗ ᓄᓇ ᐃᕐᓂᐅᖅᕝᒡᑕᐊᑦᑕᐅᖅᕐᒪᓚᐅᖅ
ᓄᑕᕐᓗᓂᖅ. ᑕᐃᒃᑯᐊ ᓄᑕᕋᖅ ᐃᓄᖕᓄᑦ ᐱᓯᒃᑐᓄᑦ
ᓇᖦᓀᖅᖦᓇᔾᐅᖅᓚᐅᖅᕐᒪᓚᐅᑦ, ᑎᒍᐊᖅᖧᖐᔪᖅᑦᑕᐊᑦᓇᑎᖦᓗ.
ᑕᐃᒃᑯᐊ ᓇᖦᓀᖅᖧᐄᓂᑦ ᐃᖑᕋᓯᖐᒥᖅ ᐅᕝᑎᔪᑦᑎᐊᖅ
ᑕᐅᑦᑐᖅᕵᑕᐅᖅᑐᑦ, ᐱᔾᐊᓂᓗ ᑕᐃᒪᐃᖕᒍᐊᖅᖤᑦᓗ ᓄᓇᒡᑦ
ᖅᑐᖅᕴᖦᓇᔾᐅᖕᒫᓇᑕᐅᖅᑐᑦ.

Way back then, there were very few Inuit in the North. So
the land started to give birth to children to help Inuit grow in
number. These babies were found and adopted by people
travelling across the tundra. When these babies grew to be
adults, they looked the same as you and I, but they were
children of the land.

ᐃᒻᒪᒃᑦᑕᒃᑕᒃᑦ ᓄᓇᖅᐸᐊᖅ ᑕᐸᐃᖏᖅᑐᖅᑲᐅᑭᔪᖃᑕᐅᖅᔾᒪᖏᖅ. ᐅᖅᑲᐅᒃᔨᑦ, ᐱᔡᑎᖅᑦ, ᐃᑯᓗᑦ ᔪᐁᖅᑦ ᑕᐸᐃᖃᓇᑕᐅᖅᔾᒪᖏᖅᑦ. ᐃᓄᐃᑦ ᔪᐁᖅᑦ ᖅᑭᒦᖅᓂᐊᖅᖃᑕᐅᖅᔾᒪᖕᑎᖅᑐᖅ. ᐃᑯᔪ ᐅᖅᑲᐅᑎᖅᐸᒍ ᓇᒍᖕᒪᐅᔾᒪᓂᖝᓂ ᐅᖕᓄᖅᖃᖝᐅᖅ, ᔾᓂᖅᑐᐃᖕᓇᐅᐅᓂᖝᐅᖝᖝᒍ, ᒻᖝᓇ ᐃᑯᔪ ᑎᖕᓯᖁᖅᑕᐅᖅᔾᒪᖏᖅ ᐅᐸᖃᑕᐅᔾᒪᔪᒡᓄ ᐃᖝᑎᖝᖁᖅᑐᓂ ᑕᑯᖝᓇᖕᔾᐊᓂᖃᐱᖝᐃᖅ ᔪᖝᓄᐊᖃᑦ ᖅᑭᓕᖝᒍᖝᖝᒍ ᖅᑭᐱᐊᖝᓂᖅᐱᐊᖅᑦ ᐃᑯᔪᓂᖝ ᖅᑯᓕᐅᖅᑐᓂᖝ ᑕᑯᖝᓂᖅᐱᐊᖅᑦ?

Way back then, there was much magic in the world. Words, objects, and even houses were magical. People did not need to travel by dog team. They would just tell their *igluit* where they wanted to be, and in the night, while everyone slept, their houses would fly to the places they were asked to go. Can you imagine looking at the night sky and seeing igluit travelling from place to place?

ᐃᒻᒪᑲᓪᓛᓗᒃ ᑕᓇᐅᖅ ᓂᕐᔪᑎᖃᑦᑎᐊᓚᐅᖅᓯᒪᙱᑦᑐᖅ. ᓇᑦᑎᖅᑕᖃᙱᑦᑐᖅ, ᕿᓚᓗᒐᖃᙱᑦᑐᖅ, ᑑᒑᓕᒃᑕᖃᙱᑦᑐᖅ, ᐊᒡᓛᓪᓘᓐᓃᑦ ᐊᐃᕙᖃᓚᐅᖅᓯᒪᙱᑦᑐᖅ. ᓄᓇᕐᔪᐊᖅ ᓄᑖᙳᑎᓪᓗᒍ ᐃᖃᓗᖃᓚᐅᖅᓯᒪᙱᑦᑐᕐᓘᓐᓃᑦ. ᑕᑯᓐᓇᙳᐊᓕᖅᐲᑦ?

ᐃᒻᒪᑲᓪᓛᓗᒃ ᐊᕐᓇᑦᑎᐊᕚᓗᒃᑕᖃᓚᐅᖅᓯᒪᔪᖅ ᐅᐃᓂᒍᒪᓱᐃᑦᑐᕐᒥᒃ. ᑕᐃᒪᐃᒃᑲᓗᐊᖅᑎᓪᓗᒍ ᓯᓚᐃᕐᓇᔭᐅᓪᓗᓂ ᐅᐃᑖᖅᑎᑕᐅᓚᐅᖅᓯᒪᔪᖅ ᑎᖕᒥᐊᑉ ᐃᓄᐊᓂᒃ. ᑖᓐᓇ ᑎᖕᒥᐊᑉ ᐃᓄᐊ ᐊᐅᓪᓚᖁᔾᔨᕗᖅ ᑖᔅᓱᒥᙵ ᐊᕐᓇᕐᒥᒃ, ᓇᓗᓇᐃᖅᓯᙱᓗᓂ ᑭᓱᓪᓚᑦᑖᖑᓂᕐᒥᓂᒃ ᐱᐅᙱᑦᑐᐊᓘᓂᕐᒥᓂᓪᓗ. ᑖᔅᓱᒪ ᐊᕐᓇᐅᑉ ᐃᓄᒐᙳᐊᑯᓗᖕᒋᓐᓂᑦ ᐊᒥᓱᑦ ᐳᐃᔩᑦ ᓵᖅᑭᓚᐅᖅᓯᒪᕗᑦ, ᑕᐃᒪᐃᓚᐅᕐᓂᖓᓄᑦ ᐅᓪᓗᒥ ᓇᑦᑎᖅᑕᐅᓕᖅᐳᖅ, ᐅᒡᔪᓪᓗ ᐊᒻᒪ ᕿᓚᓗᒐᐃᑦ.

Way back then, the sea was almost empty. There were no seal, no belugas, no narwhals, not even walruses could be found. Even fish didn't exist in the earliest days. Can you imagine that?

There was once a beautiful girl who refused to take a husband. However, one day she was tricked into marrying a bird spirit. This spirit took the woman far away from her home before revealing himself, and his cruel nature. From this woman's fingers were born many of the sea mammals we know today, such as ringed seal, bearded seal, and belugas.

"ᓄᓇᕐᔪᐊ ᑕᐃᒪᐃᑕᐅᖅᒃᖠᒪᓚᐅᖅ ᐃᒻᒃᒃᓪᓐᓐᑯᖅ," ᑕᐃᒪᓐᓇ
ᐅᖅᖅᖠᖅ ᑲᓪᔪᖅ. "ᐊᓐ ᓯᑯᒫᒥᓐᓚᑕᐅᕐᒥᐸᕐᖠᖅ ᓯᓂᓚᓯᕐᖢᓯᖢᖢ."

"ᓯᓐ ᓯᓂᒍᓐᓇᙱᓐᓇᒌᑕ. ᐅᓂᒃᖅᖣᐊᖅᕃᓐᓚᑕᐅᕐᒥᒌᑕ,"
ᓇᐃᓚ ᑭᐅᖅᖅᖅ. ᒪᒃᐸ ᐊᐃᒌᑕᐅᖅᖢᓂ ᐅᖅᑲᖠᕃᖅᖅ, "ᐊᓐ,
ᐅᓂᒃᖅᖣᐊᖅᕃᓐᓚᑕᐅᕐᒥᒌᑕ." ᑲᓪᔪᖅ ᖅᑐᖅᙱᒪᒥᓂᖅ
ᓂᐸᙱᑎᕐᖣᐊᖅ.

"ᐅᓂᒃᖅᖣᐊᖅᕃᓐᓂᒡᙱᓐᓂᐊᖅᖠᓇ.
ᐊᑭᓯᑎᐊᓚᓂᔾᖅ. ᓯᑯᒫᒥᓯᖢᖅ ᑕᑯᓇᙱᒍᐊᕐᓂᐊᖅᖹᖅ
ᐅᓂᒃᑲᐅᓯᕃᙱᒡᓚᐊᕐᓂᖅ."

"That is what the world was like way back then," said
Kudlu. "Now close your eyes, and go to sleep."

"We cannot sleep yet! Tell us more, Ataata," Nyla
replied.

Makpa yawned and added, "Yes, there must be more
to tell."

"Shhhhh," Kudlu hushed his children. "I will tell you a
bit more. Lay your heads on your pillows. Close your eyes and
try to imagine what I am telling you."

ᐃᒻᒪᒃᑦᐁᓛᓗᒃ ᐅᑭᐅᖅᑕᖅᑐᒥᐅᑕᖅᑕᖃᓚᐅᖅᓯᒪᔪᖅ ᐊᓯᑦᑎᓐᓂᒃ
ᐃᓄᐄᑦ ᓱᓕ ᑎᑭᓚᐅᖅᑎᓐᓇᒥᓂᒃ.
ᑐᓂᐅᓂᖅᑕᐅᓚᐅᖅᓯᒪᔪᖅ. ᑐᓂᑦ ᓯᓕᒃᑐᐊᔪᑦᑐᑎᒃ
ᓴᙱᑦᔭᐊᔪᑦᑐᐅᖅᓯᒪᔪᑦ, ᐃᓄᖕᓂᒃᓗ
ᐃᑦᖑᓇᐊᖅᑎᑎᑭᔪᖅᓯᖅᐸᑕᐅᖅᓯᒪᑦᑐᑎᒃ. ᐅᖃᖅᑐᖃᖅᐸᑐᖅ
ᑐᓂᒃᔫᖅ ᓴᙱᓲᐊᕐᓂᒍᓕᒃ
ᐊᐃᕕᕐᓂᕆᑎᒃ ᐃᖅᓯᒪᓗᒍ ᐊᖕᕆᖃᕐᖃᒡ ᐃᑲᔪᖅᑕᐅᙱᕆᓐᑐᓂ.
    ᑕᒫᙳᔭᐊᑕᖅᐱᔅ ᖃᓄᑎᒋ ᑐᓂᑦ
ᓴᙱᑎᑎᑕᐅᑦᓚᖕᓚᖕᕆᑦ ᐊᐃᕕᐊᑐᖕᒥᒃ ᐃᖅᓯᑎᖃᖅᑐᑎᒃ?

Way back then, there were people who lived in the North before Inuit arrived. These people were called the *Tuniit*. They were thick and strong, and they taught Inuit many things. It is even said that the Tuniit were so strong that a single hunter could carry a walrus on his back without help.

Can you imagine how strong the Tuniit must have been to do such a thing?

ᐃᒻᒪᒃᓪᓪᓗᒃ ᐅᐱᐅᖅᑕᖅᑐᖅ ᐊᒡᒥᐊᓗᖕᓂᒃ
ᓂᕐᔪᑎᕐᐊᖅᑕᐅᖅᐱᒪᕆᖅ. ᐃᖅᓯᕐᐱᐅᓂᖅᐸᖪᑕᐅᖅᐱᒪᕆᕐᑦ
ᓇᓄᕐᓗᐊᑦ, ᐊᖕᒥᕐᕐᐊᕐᓪᓗᐊᑦ ᓇᓄᐃᑦ. ᐃᒻᒪᒃᓪᓪᓗᒃ
ᖅᐸᖅᑐᖅᑐᑦ ᐅᕐᐱᖅᓯᑎᐊᓂᐊᖅᖅᐸᑕᐅᖅᐱᒪᕆᕐᑦ
ᓇᓄᕐᓗᑐᖅᖅᖃᖖᒦᖃᓗᐊᖅᒪᖕᒦᖕᒦᓗ ᑕᒫᓇ ᐃᒪᖅ ᐊᑐᖅᑕᖖᒦᑕ
ᖅᓄᒦᖕᒥᖾ.

ᑕᒻᒃᑯᐊ ᓇᓄᕐᓗᐃᑦ ᐊᖕᒥᓪᐊᕐᓂᒃᑯᓪᒋᒃ
ᐱᖅᒃᓗᖾᐅᓇᕐᓯᕐᖾᐅᕂᖃᑕᐅᖅᑐᑦ ᐳᖅᑕᑎᑦᓂᒃᕐᒋᕐᑦ. ᐅᐊᒃᓪᓕᓇᖖᒦᖦᓂᖅ,
ᓇᓄᕐᓗᐊᓗᒃ ᐱᖅᒃᓗᖾᖅᑎᑐᑦ ᐊᖕᒥᖕᒥᒋᕕᖅ?

Way back then, many giant animals lived in the North. The most feared was the *nanurluk,* the giant polar bear. Way back then, kayakers had to be watchful of these giant bears when they paddled far from land.

These bears were so big that they could be mistaken for icebergs when they floated lazily in the sea. Can you imagine a bear as large as an iceberg?

ᐃᒪᑲᓪᓚᓐᓂᒃ, ᐃᓄᒃᐸᓗᐊᖃᑕᖃᐅᒪᖅᓯᒪᔪᖅ ᓄᓇᖅᔪᐊᕐᒥ. ᐃᓄᒃᐸᓗᐊᑦ ᐊᖏᑎᒋᔭᖅᔫᐃᑦ ᐊᖃᕐᔭᐊᔅᔫᐃᑦᓗ ᐊᖅᒥᔪᐊᖅᓂᑯᓪᒃ ᓈᓐᓂᒃ ᐊᑦᔅᖃᑦᓚᐅᖅᓯᒪᔭᕐᑦ, ᑕᓄᐅᔅᔫᓗ ᐃᑉᓴᖅᓴᖅᓄᓂᒃ ᐊᖅᕕᖅᔪᐅᖅᐸᒃᓄᓂᒃ. ᓛᖁᑖ ᐃᓄᒃᐸᓗᔭᐊᔪᐃᑦ ᐃᓄᒃᐸᓗᔅᖃᑎᓐᖏᑕᓄᓪᒃ ᔪᐧᓗᓇᓄᐊᕈᖅᓗᖅᑳᑐᑕᐅᖅᓯᒪᖁᓐᑦᔮᑐᑦ, ᐅᓇᑕᕈᔭᑦᓄᓂᒃ.

᠎ ᖃᓄᖅ ᓂᐱᖃᖅᑕᖅᑐᑦᑕᐅᖅᐱᑉ ᐃᓄᒃᐸᓗᔅᑦᒃ ᐸᑦᕘᕐᓗᑎᒃᑉ? ᐃᓄᒃᐸᓗᔭᐊᔪᖅᓄᑦᒃ ᐅᓇᑕᖅᑐᖅᖃᖅᑎᓐᒥᓗ ᓂᐱᑕᐊᔪᖅᖃᑦᖅᑐᑦᖅᐅᑕᖅᓄᖅᖃᑦᒃ. ᔪᔅᓗᖃᐄ ᑲᑦᑕᖅᑐᑐᑕᐅᑦᒃ ᓂᐱᖅᖃᑦᑐᐧᑕᐅᖅᐅᖃᑦᓄᖅᖃᑦᒃ, ᐊᒻᒪᓗ ᔪᔅᓗ ᓄᓇᖅᔪᐊᖅᖃᕕᐊᒻᓄᓄᓯ.

Way back then, there were giants in the world. These huge men and women would step over rivers, and wade far into the sea to hunt for whales. These giants were usually not friendly toward each other, and would fight amongst themselves often.

What do you think it sounded like when two giants fought? I imagine it must have sounded like a thunderstorm when the giants came together. And the land must have shaken as if there were an earthquake.

ᐃᒻᒪᒃᑦᑖᓗᒃ ᐃᓄᒃᐸᓲᔮᒃᑕᖃᕋᑖᐅᖅᔭᒪᔭᖅ ᐃᓄᖕᒪ
ᑐᓐᖏᓇᖅᑐᒥᒃ. ᑖᓇ ᐃᓄᒃᐸᓲᔮᒃ ᐃᓄᑐᓐᖏᒥᒃ ᐊᖕᔭᓇᕐᑎᒥᒃ
ᑎᔾᐊᑕᐅᖅᔭᒪᔭᖅ, ᐃᕐᓂᖅᑕᓐᓪᑐᓂᐅᒃ. ᑖᒃᑯᐊᒃ ᓇᒐᑎᐁᓇᖅ
ᐱᓯᒃᑕᑕᐅᖅᔭᒪᔮᒃ ᐊᖕᔭᓇᕐᒃᐸᒃᑐᑎᓪᓗ.
         ᑕᑯᕐᓇᖕᔪᐊᑦᖅᐱᑦ ᐃᓄᑐᒃ ᐃᓄᒃᐸᓲᔮᔫᒃ ᑐᐃᓐᓂ
ᐃᒃᔾᐁᖅᑐᖅ ᓄᓇᕐᔭᒑᑦ ᑕᑯᕐᓇᕐᑐᓂ?

Way back then, there lived one huge giant who was
friendly to Inuit. This giant adopted an Inuit hunter as his
son. Together they travelled across the Arctic looking for
adventure and animals to hunt.

    Can you imagine what it must have been like for the
little hunter to sit on his giant father's shoulder and look out
onto the world?

ᐃᒻᒪᒃᑦᑖᓗᒃ, ᐃᓄᒃᐸᓱᒡᔪᐊᖕᒥᒃ ᓄᑖᖅᑖᖅᑕᖃᑐᖅᓯᒪᕗᖅ
ᓈᖅᔪᖕᒥᒃ ᐊᑎᓕᖕᒥᒃ. ᓈᖅᔪᒃ ᐃᓚᐊᕐᔪᑕᐅᖅᓯᒪᕗᖅ. ᐊᖕᔪᖅᑲᖕᒥᒋ
ᑕᒪᐅᖕᒍᔨᐊᖁᓇᖅ ᓄᓇᑐᐃᖁᓇᖕᒥ ᖅᐸᖁᔪᖅᑐᓂ ᖅᒻᒪᑯᑎᓐᑕᐅᖅᓯᒪᕗᖅ.
ᓄᓇ ᓈᖅᔪᖕᒥᒃ ᓇᒃᑐᒍᓐᑕᖕᒥ ᐊᖕᒥᖅᖅᑲᖅᑎᑎᓇᑎᓇᑕᐅᖅᓯᒪᕗᖅ
ᖅᑲᓐᖕᒥ. ᐅᖅᑲᖅᑐᖅᖅᐸᑐᖅ ᑖᓇ ᐃᓄᒃᐸᓱᒡᔪᐊᖄᕐᔪᒃ
ᓴᖕᒥᓗᐊᖅᓂᑯᓪᒃ ᖅᑲᖅᖅᒍᖕᓂᒃ ᑲᑐᓐᑎᓐᖅᑲᑦᖅᓂᖅᖅᑲᑐᒍᓂ
ᐊᖅᑭᑐᐃᖁᓇᖅᑐᓂᐅᒃ.

ᓈᖅᔪᒃ ᑕᒃᐸᓂ ᓄᐹᖕᖅ ᖅᑯᑦᖅᑎᐊᖕᕐᓂ ᓇᕿᖕᖅᑲᑐᐅᖅᑐᖅ.
ᓂᖕᒃᖕᖕᒋᒍᖅ, ᑕᐃᒪᖁ ᓄᑖᖕᖕᖕ ᓂᖕᒃᖕᖕᒋᒃ
ᖅᓄᐃᑐᐅᖁᒍᖕᖕᖅᑕᑕᖅᑐᓐᑐᖕ, ᑕᐃᒪᑐᐃᖁᓇ ᖅᓄᐃᑐᐅᖁᒍᖕᖕᕿᖕᒋ
ᐊᓄᑎᑐᖅᖕᑲᑕᐅᖅᓯᒪᕗᖅ ᐱᖅᖅᑕᖅᖅᑲᖅᑐᓂᒍ.

Way back then, there was even a baby giant named Narsuk.
Narsuk was an orphan. He had lost his parents long ago, and he
was left crying on the tundra. But the land took pity on Narsuk and
gave him the sky as his home. It is said that this baby giant is so
strong that he can knock down a mountain with a kick!

Now Narsuk lives above the clouds. And when he gets upset,
as all children do, his tantrums cause storms and blizzards.

ᐃᒻᒪᒃᑦᓴᓕᓛᖅ ᐃᓄᐃᑦ ᐊᖑᒃᑯᕚᑕᐅᖅᏁᒪᔪᕐ,
ᐊᖑᑏᓴᔭᖄᖅᓱᑎᒃ ᒥᒃᓴᔭᖄᖅᓱᑎᒡᓗ.
ᑕᐃᒪᐃᒋᐅᕐᓇᓵᔄᖅᓱᑎᒃ ᖃᓕᐊᑐᐃᐴᖄᕐᓗᑦ, ᒥᒃᓲᕐᐊᖕᖅ
ᖅᑯᐟᐊᕐᓂᖅᓯᐅᑕᐅᖅᏁᒪᔅᕙᒃ.
ᑕᐃᒪᖖᐊ ᒥᑭᔄᑯᐃᑦᑐᕐᓘᕐ, ᐊᑯᖖᓕᖁᕐᖖᓂᖅ ᑕᐃᒪᑎᒥ
ᖃᓄᖅᏁᑐᕐ ᐃᖅᏁᖅᏁᑎᒄᐅᖅᏁᒪᔪᖅ.

ᐃᓄᖃᐟᒐᖁᓄᐊᑦ ᐅᕿᐅᖅᑕᖅᑐᒌᐅᑕᐅᔄᓗᖅᏁᑦᓄᐊ
ᔅᓚ, ᐃᓄᖖᓂᖅ ᕙᖅᔾᑦᑕᐃᓕᑦᖃᑦᑕᐅᖅᏁᒪᔪᕐ.
ᑕᒌᖁᖖᒍᐊᖅᐱᖅᏁ ᐃᓄᖃᐟᒐᖁᓄᐊᑦ ᒥᑭᓄᐊᕐᖖᓂᖖᓗᐊᑦ
ᐊᖃᖅᐱᐊᑦ ᐱᑎᒪᖖᒪᖁᓄᐊᑦ ᓈᒃᑐᐊᖁᖅᐸᑕᐅᕐᖖᓂᖁᓂᖅ?

Way back then, there were magical people who could change their size whenever they wanted. And, even though they could be any size, they usually chose to stay small. For these little hunters, hunting a lemming was as dangerous as hunting a polar bear.

It is said that these little people still live in the North, but they try to avoid humans as much as they can. Can you imagine hunters so small that they could fit in the palm of your hand?

ᑲᓪᓗᒃ ᕿᑐᕐᖓᒥᓄᑦ ᕿᕕᐊᖅᐳᖅ. ᓯᑯᙱᖓᔫᒃ ᓯᓂᒃᑑᒃ ᐊᓂᖅᓵᖅᑐᑦᑎᐊᓕᖅᖢᑎᒡᓗ. ᓯᓂᓕᖅᑑᒃ.

“ᑯᓘᒃ, ᓯᓂᒃᑐᑯᓘᓕᖅᐳᓯᒃ,” ᑕᐃᒪᐃᓕᕗᖅ ᑲᓪᓗᒃ ᐃᓯᔾᔪᒃᖢᓂ. “ᐅᓂᒃᑳᖅᑐᐊᒐᒃᓴᖅᑲᕈᓐᓃᖅᑐᖓ. ᓱᕈᓯᐅᓪᓗᖓᑦᑕᐅᖅ ᓯᓂᓕᖅᐸᓚᐅᖅᓯᒪᔪᖓ ᐃᑦᑐᒃᑯᒃᑲ ᓱᓕ ᐅᓂᒃᑳᖅᑐᐊᕋᔮᖅᐸᒃᑎᑦᓗᒋᑦ.”

ᖁᖓᔅᖢᓂ ᐃᒻᒥᓄᑦ, ᑲᓪᓗᒃ ᕿᑐᕐᖓᒥᓂᒃ ᕿᐱᒃᓯᑦᑎᐊᖅᐳᖅ. ᖁᓪᓕᖅ ᒪᒥᑎᔾᔫᒥᕙᐅᒃ, ᓄᓇᖅᔪᐊᖅᑐ ᓂᐱᖅᑲᕈᓐᓃᖅᖢᓂ, ᐊᓄᕆ ᑕᖅᑳᓂ ᑐᓴᖅᓴᐅᔫᓕᖅᑐᖅ.

Kudlu looked at his children. Their eyes were closed and they were breathing softly.

"My kuluit, I am glad you are asleep," whispered Kudlu. "I didn't have much more to tell you. You see, when I was a child, I always fell asleep before my grandparents got to the end of each story, and I never heard the endings."

Smiling to himself, Kudlu made sure his children were well covered with their blankets. He dimmed the qulliq's flame, and all was quiet in the world, except for the soft whistle of the wind outside.

ᐃᑲᔪᓚᐅᖅᑐᑦ Contributors

ᔨᕐᒪᐃ ᐊᕐᓇᑦᑕᐅᔪᖅ ᐃᓅᑦᑐᓂ ᑎᑎᕋᐅᔭᖅᑎᐅᒍᖅ, ᖃᐅᔨᒪᔭᐅᓂᖅᐹᖑᑦᑐᓂᓗ ᑎᑎᕋᐅᔭᖅᑲᑦᑕᕐᓂᖓᓄᑦ, ᑎᑎᕋᐅᔭᖅᐸᒃᓱᓂᒥᑦ ᐃᓄᐃᑦ ᐅᓂᒃᑳᖅᑐᐊᖏᑦ ᐊᒻᒪ ᐃᓄᐃᑦ ᐃᒻᒪᒃᑲᓐᓂᖅ ᐃᓅᓯᕆᕙᓚᐅᖅᓯᒪᔭᖏᑦ. 2000 ᐊᕐᕌᒍ ᐊᑐᖅᑎᑦᑐᒍ, 2 ᑖᓚᐅᑉ ᑎᑎᕋᐅᔭᖅᓯᒪᓂᖓᓂᒃ ᓴᓇᓚᐅᖅᓯᒪᔪᖅ, ᑖᓐᓇ ᓇᑦᑕᐅᓐᓂᖅᓯᐅᕈᑕᐅᑦᑐᓂ ᓄᓇᕗᑦ ᐱᙱᖅᑎᑕᐅᓂᖓᓄᑦ. ᑎᑎᕋᖅᑲᑎᖅᑲᓚᐅᖅᓯᒪᖕᒥᔪᖅ ᒋᒥᒃ, ᐅᖅᑲᓕᒫᑦ ᑕᐃᔫᓯᖅᑲᖅᓱᑎᒃ ᐊᕐᓇᑦᑕᐅᔫᔪᖕᒐ: ᔨᕐᒪᐃ ᐊᕐᓇᑦᑕᐅᔫᑉ ᐃᓅᓯᖕᒐ ᐊᒻᒪ ᑎᑎᕋᐅᔭᖅᑲᑦᑕᖅᑕᖕᒥᑦ. ᔪᓗᓇᐃᕝᒥ ᓄᓇᖅᑲᖅᑐᖅ.

Germaine Arnaktauyok is an Inuit artist and illustrator, best known for her prints and etchings depicting Inuit myths and traditional ways of life. In 1999, she designed the special-edition two-dollar coin commemorating the founding of the territory of Nunavut. She is the co-author, with Gyu Oh, of *My Name is Arnaktauyok: The Life and Art of Germaine Arnaktauyok*. She lives in Yellowknife, Northwest Territories.

ᓃᑦ ᑯᕆᔅᑕᕗ ᐃᓕᓴᐃᔨᐅᔪᖅ, ᐅᖅᑲᓕᒫᒐᓕᐅᖅᑎᐅᑦᑐᓂ ᐊᒻᒪ ᑕᕐᕆᔮᒃᓴᓕᐅᖅᑎᐅᑦᑐᓂ. ᐊᕐᕌᒍᒐᓴᐅᓕᖅᑐᓄᑦ ᐅᑭᐅᖅᑕᖅᑐᒧᑦ ᓄᒃᑎᓚᐅᖅᓯᒪᔪᖅ ᐃᓕᓐᓂᐊᕐᕕᐊᓗᖕᒥ ᐃᓕᓴᖅᑕᐅᖅᑲᑦᑕᕐᓂᐊᖅᑐᓂᒃ ᐋᖅᑭᒃᓱᐃᖅᑲᑕᐅᒥᐊᖅᑐᖅᓱᓂ ᖃᐅᓯᐃᑦᑐᖅ, ᓄᓇᕗᒻᒥ. ᐃᓕᓴᖅᑎᓂᑦ ᑐᓴᖅᑲᑦᑕᓯᒥᐊᓚᐅᖅᓯᒪᔪᑦ ᐃᓅᖅᑲᑎᒋᔭᐅᖅᑲᑦᑕᖅᑐᕕᓂᕐᓂᒃ ᐃᓄᐃᑦ

ᐅᓂᒃᖅᑐᐊᖕᕐᑎᑎᔪᑦ. ᖃᐅᔨᐊᑐᑎᒥᐅᑎᐸᑦᑐᓂ ᐃᐆᔾᖕᒧ ᐊᖕᔅᐳᑎᐅᖅᕐᒥᐅᖅ.
ᐅᐱᐅᖅᑎᖅᑐᒥᐅᑎᐅᑎᖅᑐᓂ, ᓄᐊᖕᑦ ᐊᖕᑎᖕᑦᑦᑎᓂᕐᑎᓴᖅᑎᖕᖕᒪ. 16 ᐊᖕᖕᒍᑦ
ᐊᓂᒍᖅᑐᓂ, ᐆᑦ ᓄᐊᖅᖕᑎᒥᓂᖅ ᐊᒥᕐᓂᖅ ᐃᖅᖕᓇᐃᔅᖕᑎᖅᖕᖕᒃᑦᖅᖕᒥᐅᕐᒃ
ᑎᑎᖅᖕᐸᖕᑦᑎᐊᖕᑐᓂᖕᑦ ᐃᓄᐊᑦ ᐅᓂᒃᖅᑐᐊᖕᕐᑎᑦ. ᐃᖅᖕᓇᐃᔅᖕᑎᖅᖕᑐᓂ ᐃᐅᖕᐃ
ᖕᑦᐅᑎᖕᑎᒥᖅ ᐊᒥᒪ ᓄᑦᖕᒥᓂᖅ, Ćᓂ ᑯᑎᑦᑎᐅᒃᖅ, ᐆᑦ ᐅᖅᖕᑦᒪᒪᑦᖕᐅᖅᖕᐃᐊᑯᖕᒥᖅ
ᒪᐅᐃᖅᖕᒃᑕᐅᖅᖕᒥᒪᖅ ᐃᖕᓖᐊᐃᑦ ᒦᑎᐊ ᐃᖕᒃ-ᒥᖅ ᑕᐃᑦᖕᑐᐅᑎᑦ, ᐊᒪᒪ ᑕᐃᒪᖕᒪᖕᒃᓂᑦ
ᖕᖕᑦᖕᑎᑎᖕᑎᑎᖅᖕᑦᖅᑦᑎᑦᖕᑦᐅᖕᕐᔅᖕᑦᒥᕐᔅᖕᒥᖅ ᐅᐱᐅᖅᑎᖅᑐᒥᐅᑦ ᐅᓂᒃᖅᑐᐊᖕᕐᑦᒥᓂᖅ ᐊᒪᒪ
ᑎᑎᖕᑦᖕᐸᖅᑐᓂᖅ ᐅᐱᐅᖅᑎᖅᑐᒥᐅᑎᒥᖅ ᐱᔅᖕᑎᓂᒃᖕᓂᖅ.

Neil Christopher is an educator, author, and filmmaker. He first moved to the North many years ago to help start a high school program in Resolute Bay, Nunavut. It was those students who first introduced Neil to the mythical inhabitants from Inuit traditional stories. The time he spent in Resolute Bay changed the course of Neil's life. Since that first experience in the Arctic, Nunavut has been the only place he has been able to call home. For the last twenty years, Neil has worked with many community members to record and preserve traditional Inuit stories. Together with his colleague Louise Flaherty and his brother Danny Christopher, Neil started a small publishing company in Nunavut called Inhabit Media Inc., and has since been working to promote northern stories and authors.

Published in Canada by Inhabit Media Inc. (www.inhabitmedia.com)

Inhabit Media Inc. (Iqaluit Office) P.O. Box 11125, Iqaluit, Nunavut, X0A 1H0 • (Toronto Office) 146A Orchard View Blvd., Toronto, Ontario, M4R 1C3

Design and layout copyright © 2015 Inhabit Media Inc.
Text copyright © 2015 by Neil Christopher
Illustrations by Germaine Arnaktauyok copyright © 2015 Inhabit Media Inc.

Editor: Louise Flaherty
Art Director: Neil Christopher

We acknowledge the support of the Canada Council for the Arts for our publishing program.
We acknowledge the support of the Government of Canada through the Department of Canadian Heritage Canada Book Fund program.

Printed and bound in the United States.

ISBN 978-1-77227-021-1
Library and Archives Canada Cataloguing in Publication

Christopher, Neil, 1972-, author
        Taiksumanialuk / titiraqtat Niil Kuristavumut ; titiraujaqtat Jirmai
Arnattaujurmut = Way back then / written by Neil Christopher ; illustrated
by Germaine Arnaktauyok.

Title in Inuktitut romanized.
Text in Inuktitut (in syllabic characters) and English; translated from
    the English.
ISBN 978-1-77227-021-1 (bound)

        1. Giants--Juvenile fiction. 2. Animals--Juvenile fiction.
I. Arnaktauyok, Germaine, illustrator II. Christopher, Neil, 1972- . Way
back then. III. Christopher, Neil, 1972- . Way back then. Inuktitut.
IV. Title. V. Title: Way back then.

PS8605.H7548W291548 2015   jC813'.6   C2015-902961-9